A Note to Parents and Caregivers:

Read-it! Readers are for children who are just starting on the amazing road to reading. These beautiful books support both the acquisition of reading skills and the love of books.

 The PURPLE LEVEL presents basic topics and objects using high frequency words and simple language patterns.

 The RED LEVEL presents familiar topics using common words and repeating sentence patterns.

 The BLUE LEVEL presents new ideas using a larger vocabulary and varied sentence structure.

 The YELLOW LEVEL presents more challenging ideas, a broad vocabulary, and wide variety in sentence structure.

 The GREEN LEVEL presents more complex ideas, an extended vocabulary range, and expanded language structures.

 The ORANGE LEVEL presents a wide range of ideas and concepts using challenging vocabulary and complex language structures.

When sharing a book with your child, read in short stretches, pausing often to talk about the pictures. Have your child turn the pages and point to the pictures and familiar words. And be sure to reread favorite stories or parts of stories.

There is no right or wrong way to share books with children. Find time to read with your child, and pass on the legacy of literacy.

Adria F. Klein, Ph.D.
Professor Emeritus
California State University
San Bernardino, California

To my friend Marisol, and to all children who are learning to read

First American edition published in 2005 by
Picture Window Books
5115 Excelsior Boulevard
Suite 232
Minneapolis, MN 55416
877-845-8392
www.picturewindowbooks.com

First published in Canada in 1999 by
Les éditions Héritage inc.
300 Arran Street, Saint Lambert
Quebec, Canada J4R 1K5

Printed in the United States of America.

Library of Congress Cataloging-in-Publication Data
Papineau, Lucie.
Bamboo at jungle school / Lucie Papineau ; [illustrated by] Dominique Jolin.
p. cm. — (Read-it! readers)
Summary: Betty, a young monkey, receives a little man, Bamboo, as a gift, but when she takes the bus to jungle school, her devoted but lonely friend visits the classroom with unexpected results.
ISBN 1-4048-1036-6 (hardcover)
[1. Monkeys—Fiction. 2. Jungles—Fiction. 3. Schools—Fiction. 4. Friendship—Fiction.]
I. Jolin, Dominique, ill. II. Title. III. Series.

PZ7.P2115Bam 2004
[E]—dc22   2004023772

Bamboo at Jungle School

By Lucie Papineau
Illustrated by Dominique Jolin

Special thanks to our advisers for their expertise:

Adria F. Klein, Ph.D.
Professor Emeritus, California State University
San Bernardino, California

Susan Kesselring, M.A.
Literacy Educator
Rosemount - Apple Valley - Eagan (Minnesota) School District

PICTURE WINDOW BOOKS
Minneapolis, Minnesota

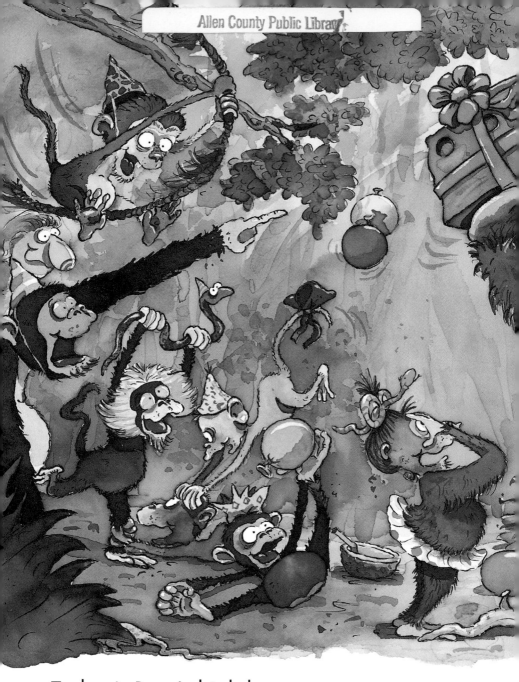

Today is Betty's birthday.

Her father gives her a wonderful present.

Look! It's a little man. His name is Bamboo.

Betty loves her present.

The little man loves Betty. He follows
her everywhere.

This morning, Betty is going to Jungle School.

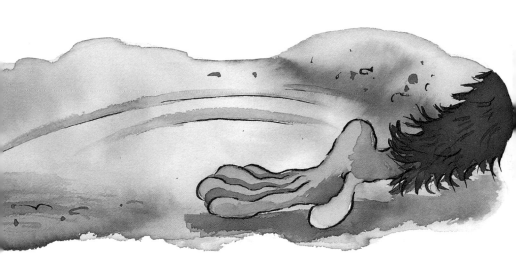

Betty climbs onto the school bus.

Bamboo climbs on, too.

Betty goes to school with her friends.

Bamboo is all alone. He has nothing to do.

Bamboo wants to go to school, too.

He climbs up the tree where Betty is sitting.

The teacher forgot his glasses. He thinks
Bamboo is a new student.

"Sit down!" says the teacher. "It's time for today's lesson: fleas."

The monkeys stop monkeying around. Bamboo
does, too, even though he's not a monkey.

18

The first lesson is to look for fleas in your friends' fur.

Bamboo can't play. He doesn't have any
fur at all!

The second lesson is to catch a flea between your fingers.

Bamboo is sad. He doesn't have a single flea.

The third lesson is to swallow the flea in a single gulp.

Yuck! Bamboo hates the taste of fleas!

The fourth lesson is to learn to count fleas.

"How many fleas are there?" asks the teacher.

All the little monkeys scratch their heads.

Bamboo counts. And counts again.

"There are exactly eight fleas, sir,"
Bamboo says.

The little monkeys clap their paws.

Bamboo loves Jungle School. And Betty really loves her little Bamboo.

More *Read-it!* Readers

Bright pictures and fun stories help you practice your reading skills. Look for more books at your level.

Bamboo at Jungle School by Lucie Papineau
The Best Snowman by Margaret Nash
Bill's Baggy Pants by Susan Gates
Cleo and Leo by Anne Cassidy
Felix on the Move by Maeve Friel
I Am in Charge of Me by Dana Meachen Rau
Jasper and Jess by Anne Cassidy
The Lazy Scarecrow by Jillian Powell
Let's Share by Dana Meachen Rau
Little Joe's Big Race by Andy Blackford
The Little Star by Deborah Nash
Meg Takes a Walk by Susan Blackaby
The Naughty Puppy by Jillian Powell
Selfish Sophie by Damian Kelleher

Looking for a specific title or level? A complete list of *Read-it!* Readers is available on our Web site: *www.picturewindowbooks.com*